The Only Puppy

By Ginny Musante Erickson

Illustrations by Christina Cartwright

Dedication

This book is dedicated to anyone who has
ever felt lonely or misunderstood.

Goldie, the retriever, had been expecting pups for weeks.

But when the special day came, only
one pup was delivered.

"Where are all the others?"
said the mother to her pup.

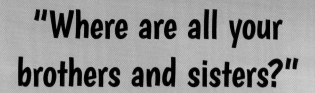

"It's only me," said the only puppy.

"Who will you play with?" asked Goldie.

"I could play with you."

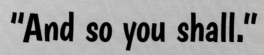

"And so you shall."

For the next six weeks,

Goldie fed and groomed...

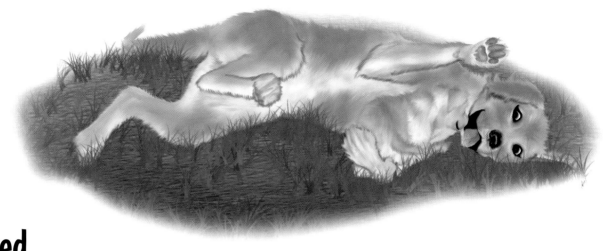

and played...

and played...

and played with her
only puppy.

And the only
puppy grew...

and
grew...

and grew.

Until one day she was big enough to go home with a family.

"Play with me, play with me,"
said the only puppy.

"No barking,"
said the father.

"Play with me, play with me,"
said the only puppy.

"No jumping," said the mother.

"Play with me, play with me,"
said the only puppy.

"No biting," said the children.

The only puppy was lonely.

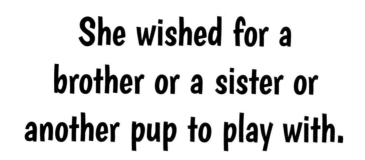

She wished for a
brother or a sister or
another pup to play with.

And when she opened her eyes, she saw one in the window.

"Play with me, play with me," said the only puppy as she danced and wagged her tail.

"Play with me, play with me," said the only puppy when she saw her new friend in the kitchen.

"Play with me, play with me," said the only puppy as she splashed at her buddy in her water bowl.

"Stop splashing!" said the father.

"There's no puppy in your water bowl," said the mother.

"It's only your reflection,"
said the children.

The only puppy was lonely again and again she wished for another pup to play with.

She looked
in her water
bowl.

She looked
in the
kitchen.

And when she looked out the window,
her wish had come true.

Another puppy had moved in next door.

And the only puppy
wasn't lonely anymore.

Balboa Press books may be ordered through booksellers or by contacting:

Balboa Press
A Division of Hay House
1663 Liberty Drive
Bloomington, IN 47403
www.balboapress.com
1 (877) 407-4847

Because of the dynamic nature of the Internet, any web addresses or links contained in this book may have changed since publication and may no longer be valid. The views expressed in this work are solely those of the author and do not necessarily reflect the views of the publisher, and the publisher hereby disclaims any responsibility for them.

ISBN: 978-1-4525-8656-4 (hc)
ISBN: 978-1-4525-8655-7 (e)

Library of Congress Control Number: 2013920456

Balboa Press rev. date: 07/23/2014

Printed in the United States by Bookmasters
Ashland, OH
September 2014
50006405

BALBOA.
PRESS
A DIVISION OF HAY HOUSE